The Smallest Kitten

Other titles by Holly Webb

The Smallest Kitten

Holly Webb

Illustrated by Sophy Williams

LiTTLE TiGER

LONDON

For twins – and parents of twins – everywhere!

STRIPES PUBLISHING LIMITED
An imprint of the Little Tiger Group
1 Coda Studios, 189 Munster Road, London SW6 6AW

Imported into the EEA by Penguin Random House Ireland,
Morrison Chambers, 32 Nassau Street, Dublin D02 YH68

A paperback original
First published in Great Britain in 2022

Text copyright © Holly Webb, 2022
Illustrations copyright © Sophy Williams, 2022
Author photograph © Charlotte Knee Photography

ISBN: 978-1-78895-389-4

MIX
Paper from
responsible sources
FSC® C171272
www.fsc.org

The Forest Stewardship Council® (FSC®) is a global, not-for-profit
organization dedicated to the promotion of responsible forest management
worldwide. FSC defines standards based on agreed principles for
responsible forest stewardship that are supported by environmental, social,
and economic stakeholders. To learn more, visit www.fsc.org

10 9 8 7 6 5 4 3 2 1

Chapter One

Amina raced up the steps at the front of the animal shelter and twirled round and round in front of the door. "Come on!" she called to the rest of the family. "Zara! Hurry up! Don't you want to see the kittens?"

Zara didn't dash after her twin sister. She pushed her hand into Dad's instead, holding on to him tight. She wanted to go and meet the kittens, of course she did. It was just that she was excited in a different way. She didn't do dancing about like Amina did. Her excitement was all inside, but it was definitely there. She and Amina had been talking about this moment for so long – imagining meeting their very own kitten for the first time.

Zara slipped the hand that wasn't holding Dad's into her pocket, closing it around the folded printout that she'd been carrying about for days, ever since Mum had emailed the animal shelter to say they were interested in the kittens. Zara had got her to print one of the photos, so she could keep looking at it. It showed all three kittens snuggled up in a soft cat bed, two tabby ones mostly on top of a little black-and-white one. She didn't seem to mind though. She looked quite comfy with a warm blanket of kitten on top of her.

"Excited?" Mum leaned over to look at Zara, smiling. "I know how much you've been looking forward to this."

Zara nodded hard and smiled back, but she still didn't say anything.

Up at the top of the steps, Amina was tugging open the heavy glass door…

When Mum and Dad had told the girls they would be able to go and see the kittens and choose which one they wanted to adopt, Zara had thought they'd only be allowed to look at them, maybe through a door into their pen. But instead they were taken to a special meeting room and James, the man who worked at the shelter, explained to them that they just needed to wait while he went to fetch the kittens.

"Do you think we'll get to hold them?" Zara asked Mum hopefully as James hurried off.

Amina nodded. "Look! There are cat toys in that basket. I think we can play with the kittens."

Zara looked round and saw a basket full of all different sorts of toys – balls, feathery birds, squishy mice… Just the kind of things she'd been thinking of buying with her pocket money, ever since Mum and Dad had said they could get a kitten when they'd moved to their new house.

Zara and Amina's mum had recently changed jobs. She now worked at a hospital that was too far away for her to commute. It was a huge change for everyone – Amina and Zara would have to start at a different school too. But there were some good things about moving. Mum and Dad had always said their old house was too small for pets, and it was by a busy road. The new house had a garden and it was really quiet. Perfect for a cat. Amina and Zara were going to be ten soon – ten was definitely old enough to look after a pet, and they'd promised to help lots. Mum and Dad had promised they would contact the animal shelter as soon as they'd settled in. Even though it had only been a couple of weeks, it felt like a very long wait...

"Is he coming back yet?" Amina asked, bouncing up from her chair.

"It won't be long," Mum said, laughing at her.

Dad turned to the door. "I think I can hear them, actually."

The girls stared hopefully at the

door – and Dad was right. James eased it open and stepped through with a cat carrier. Tiny, squeaky, cross little mews echoed from inside, until James set the carrier down and opened the wire door, and then there was a curious silence. Amina and Zara exchanged a wide-eyed look and Amina slipped her hand into Zara's. After all the waiting…

Two small tabby faces appeared at the door of the carrier and Zara caught her breath. Even Amina was too excited to speak – or perhaps she'd realized she needed to be quiet and let the kittens work up the courage to come out. The two kittens watched the room for a moment, their whiskers twitching. Then one of them padded out of the carrier – he was small enough that it was a big step down to the floor. He stumbled across the tiles to sniff at Amina's sandals.

"Mum!" Amina breathed, her eyes shining. "Look! He's tickling me!" She giggled and twitched, and the kitten play-pounced on the fabric flowers on her shoes. The second tabby kitten tumbled after the first one, eager to see what this exciting new game was.

James laughed and handed Amina a feathery toy. "Try this instead, otherwise your sandals might never be the same again." He smiled at Zara and offered her the basket of toys.

Zara took out a squishy toy fish and sat holding it, wondering if the kittens would come and investigate her too. But they were too interested in the feather wand that Amina was bouncing up and down. The two kittens looked like wind-up toys, turning their heads every time she wobbled the feathers. Mum and Dad and Amina were laughing delightedly, and Zara laughed too, even though she felt just a tiny bit jealous. She didn't want to take the kittens away from Amina – she only wished they'd play with her as well.

Then Zara glanced round, her attention caught by the smallest movement over by the carrier. Of course! There was another kitten! Zara had been so caught up watching the two tabby kittens that she'd forgotten about the little black-and-white girl. She was just stepping cautiously out of the carrier, trying to get down over the edge of the door.

Zara bit her lip as the kitten padded around with one paw, trying to work out how far down the floor was. She was definitely smaller than the tabbies and Zara was worried she might not be able to get out. But eventually the kitten bumped down on to the tiles and stopped to look around again. Zara didn't know very much about cats – not yet – but she could tell the kitten wasn't nearly as confident and bouncy as her brother and sister. Maybe she was shy?

Zara was quite used to people talking about her as "the shy twin", or "the quiet one". People said it all the time, even though Mum and Dad tried to tell them not to. Only a couple of days ago, Dad had persuaded Amina to walk down to the shops with him, while Mum kept Zara behind to have a "little chat". Mum wanted to talk to her about the new school they were going to after the summer holidays, and about trying to make friends, and not letting Amina do all the talking. Zara had listened, of course she had, and nodded in all the right places and promised Mum she'd try. But it wasn't as easy as that. At their old school, Amina had done all the friend-making, and Zara didn't mind. It made things easier when Amina talked for her. Sometimes she did wish she had a best friend of her own though – as well as her twin, of course.

How do you make friends? Amina wondered as she watched the little black-and-white kitten tiptoe towards her. Perhaps it was just about being brave enough to go up to someone.

"Hey…" she whispered as the kitten paused to sniff thoughtfully at the lace of her trainer and then bat the trailing end with one paw.

The kitten stopped, staring up at
her worriedly, and Zara stared back.
She waited for the kitten to dash
back to the carrier, but she didn't. She
was too interested in Zara's shoelace.
Carefully, Zara jiggled her foot. Not
too hard – she didn't want to hurt the
kitten – but just enough to make her
lace bounce up and down.

The kitten watched fixedly, her green eyes round – and then she pounced, flinging herself at the loose shoelace and scrabbling at it with all four paws.

Zara desperately wanted to laugh, but she held it in so she didn't scare the kitten away. She just watched, grinning to herself, as the kitten stalked her shoelace over and over again.

After a couple of minutes, the kitten seemed to decide she wanted to explore a little further. She'd flung herself right on top of Zara's trainer with her last leap, and now she wriggled and stumbled her way up Zara's leg, her tiny claws hooking into Zara's jeans.

Zara watched delightedly, hardly able to believe there was a kitten climbing into her lap. She stood on

Zara's knee for a moment, watching Amina playing with her brother and sister, and then she turned around and slumped down.

"Zara..." Mum whispered from across the room. "You found the other kitten!"

"She found me," Zara whispered back. "She was playing with my shoelace."

"Oh, look at her," Amina said admiringly. "She's so little and cute."

"You know," Dad said thoughtfully. "I wonder if these tabby kittens belong together, they seem such good friends. We only wanted to get one cat..."

Zara looked up at him, her eyes hopeful. "Please can we take this little one home?"

19

Chapter Two

The kitten curled up at the back of the carrier. Hopefully she would be safe in here. Everything outside was strange and different. She couldn't hear the noises she was used to – her brother and sister, the cats in the pens close by, even dogs a bit further away. There were no familiar smells either. She couldn't smell any other cats at all. She didn't remember being the only cat, not ever.

She didn't like it. When she'd been put in the carrier she'd hoped to find her brother and sister again. They had disappeared a couple of days earlier, and the black-and-white kitten had been waiting anxiously for them to come back. She was sure they weren't here though, she would have smelled them.

She pressed herself tighter against the back wall of the carrier, listening to the noises around. There were heavy footsteps, and lighter ones, and voices.

"Can't we get her out?"

"I think we should leave it to her. She's scared, Amina. You would be too. She's only little."

"I know… But it's been ages. I want to play with her."

"I expect she'll come out when she's hungry." That was a deeper voice. "She just needs time. She was enjoying playing with us at the shelter the other day, wasn't she, Zara? She's a friendly little thing. She doesn't know what's going on right now. We don't want to scare her any more. Let's put some food down and let her come out when she feels like it."

There was a sigh and then the first voice said, "I suppose."

The kitten's ears twitched as she heard a familiar sound – biscuits rattling against the side of a bowl. She'd heard that noise often at the shelter, when someone brought their food. She was hungry. Still nervous, but hungry... She crept a few steps forwards and caught the scent of biscuits, just like the ones she was used to.

"Just sit back a bit, girls. Give her a chance to come out without having to get too close."

The voice sounded gentle and whoever was speaking wasn't right up by the door of the carrier. The kitten approached the door and looked out cautiously. There were four people watching her – two girls sitting on the floor, someone else sitting by the table and another person standing up, putting away a bag that probably had the food in it. The food smelled so delicious. She measured the distance

to the food bowl in her head. It was
close – she could dart out and eat, and
if anything frightening happened, she
would whip straight back to the carrier
where it was safe. She could feel all
those eyes staring straight at her and
she wasn't sure about it at all.

The kitten hopped out of the carrier and hurried across to the bowl, bolting down the food as fast as she could, while keeping an eye on all the people in the room. They were still staring but they didn't move and no one tried to grab her. The kitten began to relax, eating more slowly. At last, she finished the bowl of biscuits, licking up the crumbs and sniffing around hopefully in case there was more. But the bowl was definitely empty.

She sat back, eyeing the family thoughtfully and swiping a paw across her whiskers. They had fed her when she was hungry. It didn't mean she trusted them, not yet – but it was a start. She finished cleaning her whiskers and looked at the girl she'd slept on, back at the shelter.

"Don't stare at her," the girl whispered to the other one, who was sitting next to her on the floor. "I don't think she likes it."

"How do you know?"

"I just don't think she does. Please, Amina…"

"OK, OK."

Both the girls looked down at the floor at exactly the same time and the kitten gave a little jump of surprise. They seemed to move in the same way, these two. Curiously she padded towards them, sniffing at their outstretched toes and then nudging the side of her chin against their feet. Both girls twitched and giggled, and the kitten darted back. But then they settled again and she went back to investigating. That big bowl of food had made her feel sleepy and she wanted to curl up somewhere soft and warm – a basket, or a lap, perhaps.

The first girl stretched out her hand and ran it very gently over the kitten's back. That was nice. Soothing... The kitten hopped up on to her leg and kneaded at the girl's soft skirt with her paws. There was a dip, a little hollow that looked comfy, and she settled herself into it, turning herself round and round until she was nestled into the gap between the two girls' legs.

"I think we should call her Cola," Amina said firmly. "Mum, don't you think that would be a good name? She looks like a Cola."

Zara looked lovingly down at the black-and-white kitten, who was now curled up in the soft igloo bed they'd bought from the pet shop. She and Amina had kept as still as they could when the kitten had curled up in between them, but eventually they'd had to move.

Mum had scooped the kitten up and laid her gently in the basket, and she hadn't even woken up properly. She'd made a snuffly little noise and huddled into the side of the cat bed. Cola was a cute name, but it didn't seem quite right. And Zara wanted their kitten to be called something perfect.

"No."

Amina swung round, her eyes wide with surprise. "No?"

"I don't think she looks like a Cola. A cat called Cola ought to be all black. Our kitten's got a white front and white paws."

Amina still looked shocked but Mum smiled. "What would be a good name, then?"

"Maybe something that shows how little she is?" Zara suggested.

Amina shook her head. "That won't work. Of course she's little now, she's only a kitten. But she's going to grow, isn't she?"

"I know that!" Zara could hear herself arguing, and it was very surprising, as though she was listening to someone else talk, a bit like watching a film. She almost never argued with her twin, it was just easier not to. Amina was louder and more confident than Zara – she always had been, even when they were babies, Dad said. Arguing with her twin just made Zara sad so she didn't – unless it was really important. Like now. "But she was much littler than the two tabby kittens. I think she's always going to be small, and she's got really big, pointy ears too. They didn't have those. So – so I think she looks like an elf. We should call her Elfie – no! Pixie!" She swallowed hard and saw that Mum was still beaming at her.

"That's a very sweet name. She does look like a little pixie. I think it would suit her when she's bigger too."

"I like it," Dad said.

"I suppose," Amina agreed, even though she didn't sound very certain. "It is cute… Oh, look, she's waking up! Hey, Pixie-Cola…" She darted a look at Zara, as if she were daring her to argue, but Zara was too pleased that she'd made Amina listen to mind.

"She's going exploring," she murmured happily, watching as the kitten stretched and sniffed, and then began to wander slowly around the kitchen. She found the new litter tray they'd bought and weed in it, which was good, even though it was a bit yucky to think about clearing it out. Better there than puddles on the floor, though. Mum and Dad looked relieved.

"Oh, where's she going?" Amina asked, watching as the kitten pushed her way under the trolley where Dad kept the vegetables. The kitten wriggled right underneath and then popped out again to explore the tiny space behind the recycling bin. After that she settled down behind the wellies by the back door for a few minutes. Amina giggled and nudged Zara. "She's just like you."

"What do you mean?" Zara blinked
at her, confused.

"Hiding. You're always doing it.
Remember when you went and hid in
the bathroom cupboard and fell asleep,

and Mum got in a total panic?"

Dad snorted with laughter and Zara saw Mum giving him a cross look. She felt her cheeks burn. She did like to hide herself away in small, quiet places, especially if she was feeling sad or shy. She wished Amina hadn't said anything…

Pixie crept out from behind the wellies and sat down on Zara's foot with a huge yawn. Zara wasn't sure how she could be sleepy again when she'd only just woken up, but then she had done quite a lot of exploring for someone so small. Carefully, she reached down and scooped the kitten up, snuggling her against her T-shirt. Zara wasn't really sure if Pixie would stay but she'd liked being curled up on

her and Amina before,
hadn't she? And right
now, Zara felt sad and
hurt, and she wanted
someone to cuddle.
Maybe the kitten
wanted a cuddle too?

She did look a
bit surprised for a
moment, but then
she yawned again and
slumped over Zara's arm,
soft and saggy.

It was the nicest thing
Zara could remember
happening, ever.

Chapter Three

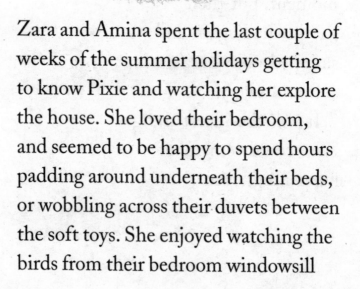

Zara and Amina spent the last couple of weeks of the summer holidays getting to know Pixie and watching her explore the house. She loved their bedroom, and seemed to be happy to spend hours padding around underneath their beds, or wobbling across their duvets between the soft toys. She enjoyed watching the birds from their bedroom windowsill too. Zara thought that she was going to love going out in the garden when she was a bit older and she'd had her vaccinations.

Dad was keen to take Amina and Zara out to look around the town – there was a swimming pool and a cinema, even a bowling alley. But neither of the girls wanted to leave Pixie for long.

"She'll be lonely," Zara explained on their way back from getting their library cards. She had a huge pile of books and was planning to turn her duvet into a tent over the top of her bed and read them all. Maybe she could persuade Pixie into the tent too… The good thing about Amina being so bouncy and energetic was that she liked to dance around and get Pixie to chase her toys. Then once the kitten was properly worn out, she'd snuggle up and snooze while Zara stroked her.

"I expect she hasn't even woken up from her after-breakfast sleep," Dad said. "Cats sleep for about sixteen hours a day, did you know that? Pixie's going for the record, I think."

"She's not lazy, Dad," Zara protested. "Haven't you seen her jumping after her feather toy?"

"And she's growing," Amina put in. "She's much bigger than she was a week ago. Her coat's different too, she's not as fluffy. She's turning silky instead."

Zara nodded, realizing that Amina was right. "You'd sleep all the time if you had to do all that growing, Dad."

"I know, I'm only teasing. Anyway, I think you two are going to be the experts on kittens, with all the cat books you've borrowed." He looked thoughtfully at the shops they were passing. "Is there anything we need to get for school?"

"New lunchboxes?" Amina asked hopefully, looking at the Back to School display in the window.

"What's wrong with the one you've got?" Dad asked and Amina shrugged.

"Nothing, I'd just like a new one!"

Zara looked at the school supplies too, suddenly feeling the weight of all the library books in the bag she was carrying. It was only a week now until they started their new school. They'd be going into Year Five, which meant that everyone else would have known each other for years and years. She really wasn't very good at getting to know new people.

Dad nudged her gently. "What about you, Zara? Need anything? Do you want to get a new lunchbox?"

Zara shook her head. "No…" she whispered. "I'd just like everything to stay the same."

Back at the house, Zara found Pixie still sleeping in her igloo bed in the kitchen and she lay down on the floor next to her, peering in. Pixie was asleep on her back, showing off her tummy. Zara stroked the soft white fur with one finger, and Pixie stretched a little and let out a breathy purr.

"I'd forgotten how close it was to school starting," Zara murmured. "I've been too busy looking after you to think about it." She stroked one of

Pixie's tiny paws and sighed. "I wish I could just curl up in a furry nest all day. Or hide under all the toys at the end of my bed, like you do when Dad shouts up the stairs." Zara smiled, remembering Pixie's tail poking out from underneath her toy octopus like an extra tentacle. Amina had been right about Pixie and Zara both liking small, dark spaces. Pixie definitely felt safe when she was somewhere dark and quiet and so did Zara. "Amina's totally different," Zara pointed out to the sleeping kitten. "I think maybe she just gets louder when she's feeling worried…" She sighed. "I'm going to miss you so much…"

"Be good, Pixie," Zara whispered, cuddling the little kitten against her stiff new uniform cardigan as Amina raced around trying to work out where she'd left her pencil case. "At least we've only got to do three days this first week, and then it'll be the weekend. I'll see you this afternoon when I get back. Wish me luck." She smiled faintly as Pixie nudged her cheek and purred – her purr was so huge for such a little cat.

"Time to go, girls." Dad smiled at them encouragingly. "We want to be nice and early on your first day."

One of the good things about moving was that their house was really close to their new school, only about a ten-minute walk. Once they were settled

in, Amina and Zara might even be able
to walk by themselves. Zara supposed
it was good to be a bit closer – but right
now she didn't want to be at school at
all. It didn't help that they soon started
to spot other children in the dark green
uniform. There were some girls who
looked like they might be in Year Five
too, all walking together and chatting
and giggling. Zara was sure they were
pointing her and Amina out and talking
about them. She *hated* people noticing
her. Now it was going to be happening
all day.

Once they arrived at the school, they
seemed to be swept up and away into a
tide of niceness – the school secretary,
and then the head teacher, and then
their class teacher, all smiling and

saying how good it was to have them there. Amina beamed and chattered about their old school and their move, and Zara managed a small, tight smile.

The two girls were sitting next to each other close to the front of the room when the rest of the class came in.

"Shh, sit down, everyone, please." Miss Modha smiled around at them. "I hope everyone had a great summer." She nodded to the twins. "We're lucky to have Zara and Amina joining our class this year."

Zara stared at the table, feeling her cheeks redden. Out of the corner of her eye, she could see Amina waving and smiling around the class.

"Which is which?" someone whispered.

"I'm Amina. And we're not identical, but if you can't tell, I've got a ponytail and Zara has a plait. We always do our hair that way."

Zara drew her plait over her shoulder, fiddling with the end. It gave her fingers something to do.

"That's very helpful, Amina. Would you two like to tell us something about yourselves? Only if you want to, of course!"

"We've just moved to Stallbridge and our mum's a doctor at the hospital," Amina went on. "Oh, and two weeks ago we got a kitten! She's black and white and her name's Pixie. Have you still got her photo?" she added to Zara, and Zara pulled it out of her pocket and handed it over. She'd stopped carrying it around once they'd brought Pixie home, but today she'd put it in the pocket of her school skirt, for comfort. Amina held the photo up and Miss Modha leaned over to look.

"So cute! She looks tiny. Lucky you, having a kitten."

"Does your sister talk?" One of the girls on the other side of their table asked, nodding to Zara. Zara looked down again swiftly, biting her lip.

"Thank you, Amina," Miss Modha put in quickly. "You'll all have lots of time to chat to Zara and Amina at break time. For now we need to get on with giving out books. Find a pen, all of you, and I've put how I want you to name your books up on the whiteboard."

Half the morning disappeared in fiddly first-day tasks and the bell for break rang far too soon for Zara.

Several girls gathered around them as Miss Modha shooed them out into the playground, asking questions about their old school and generally being curious.

"I really like your hairband," one of the girls said to Zara.

"Oh, thanks." She tried desperately to think of something nice to say back. Mum had said it would be easy – she just had to say the same sort of thing the person talking had said. Mum called it echoing. But the girl smiling at her had short hair, with no clips or bands in it at all. Zara stared at her helplessly and the girl turned to listen to Amina telling a funny story about their old teacher at Springfield Primary who could never remember which of them was which.

"And it's not like it's difficult!" she finished off, nodding over at Zara as if to say how different they were. Everyone laughed – because already, after only half a morning, they could see that the twins were nothing like each other at all.

Zara tried to laugh and join in the joke, but it just hurt too much.

"Hey… I loved your kitten."

Zara jumped and looked round. She'd been trying so hard to be part of the laughing group she hadn't noticed the girl standing beside her.

"And Pixie's such a sweet name.

Here, do you want
to see my cat?"
She held up
a keyring, the
kind you could
put a photo
inside. It had
a very large,
very fluffy, very
orange cat on
it. The cat was
lying on its
back, showing
off a cream and
orange stripey
tummy. It looked a bit like a rug.

"He's gorgeous!" Zara said, before
she'd even had time to think. "Um, is
he a he? The cat book I got from the

library said most ginger cats were."

"Yup. He's called Biscuit – like ginger biscuit?"

"That's clever!" Zara beamed at the other girl and then realized she was actually talking to someone without Amina helping her. She had a split second of panic and then thought that it didn't matter, because there was something she actually did want to know.

"What's your name?"

Pixie wandered from the living room along the hall and into the kitchen – again. She'd been back and forth all morning, trying to work out where

Zara and Amina had gone. They'd disappeared before, but never for this long.

"Hey, little one." Dad came out of the office next to the kitchen and crouched down to tickle her behind the ears. Pixie rubbed herself around his ankles but he wasn't the one she was looking for. It was the girls she was missing.

"They'll be back later," Dad murmured, smiling as Pixie plodded determinedly down the hallway again. This time she stopped and looked up at the stairs. Amina and Zara were up there sometimes and they'd pick her up and take her with them too. Maybe that's where they were? She put her front paws on the bottom step, stretching and trying to peer up at the top of the stairs. She couldn't *hear* them…

Her sharp ears caught a faint crunching on the gravel outside the front door and she turned to look – and then jumped wildly as the doorbell rang.

"It's OK, don't panic. I know, it's so loud, isn't it?" Dad said as he hurried to answer the door to the friendly woman who delivered the post. He looked round carefully to make sure he wasn't accidentally going to let Pixie out, but he couldn't see her anywhere.

Pixie was crouched, trembling, under the potted palm tree at the bottom of the stairs – the pot stood

on three little legs and if she squeezed
tight enough, she could just about get
underneath. Down there it was dark
and shadowy and safe...

Chapter Four

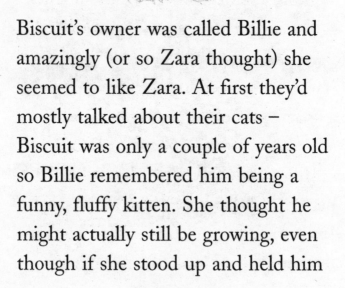

Biscuit's owner was called Billie and amazingly (or so Zara thought) she seemed to like Zara. At first they'd mostly talked about their cats – Biscuit was only a couple of years old so Billie remembered him being a funny, fluffy kitten. She thought he might actually still be growing, even though if she stood up and held him under his front paws, the tip of his tail trailed on the floor.

"I think he must be about six times the size of Pixie," Zara told her seriously that first break time. "Amina says Pixie's going to get a lot bigger but I'm not sure. She just feels like she's going to stay small forever."

Billie looked thoughtfully over at Amina, perched on one of the picnic tables in the playground, surrounded by a giggling crowd of girls. "Your sister talks a lot, doesn't she?"

Zara felt her face grow hot and she stared down at the photo of Pixie.

Billie leaned over to look at her better. "I didn't mean it in a bad way! It's just – she's right, isn't she? You're really not that similar." She sighed.

"Sorry. I get into trouble for saying stuff because people think I'm being mean. I'm not. Mum says I should count to five and think before I say anything, but who's got time for that?"

Zara snorted with surprised

laughter and Billie grinned at her. "See? You know I'm right."

"Amina never stops talking…" Zara admitted. "Usually I don't mind. But…" Billie looked at her curiously. Zara swallowed and went on, "But it's nice to talk for myself sometimes." She smiled shyly at Billie and remembered something her mum had mentioned the day before. "Um… It's our birthday in a couple of weeks." She took a deep breath. "Do you want to come to our party?"

Zara hadn't been very excited about having a birthday party when Mum had first mentioned it, but it turned out Amina had been making plans. On Friday evening after school, she hurried Zara upstairs to change out of their uniform and then back down to talk to their parents. Mum had just finished her shift at the hospital and Dad was making dinner.

Zara felt more like lying on the sofa with Pixie than discussing birthday plans – even just three days at their new school had worn her out. Still, looking back on it, the first week had gone a lot better than she'd thought it would – and a big part of that had been finding her own friend. Miss Modha had even asked her if she'd like to move tables and sit with Billie. Zara had said yes before she thought about what it would mean – that she wouldn't be sitting with Amina.

She thought Amina had looked a bit shocked when she told her.

Now she sat down at the table, yawning, and twitched the tail on her leopard onesie for Pixie to chase.

"We've been thinking about our party," Amina announced. Zara looked up, feeling a bit irritated. They hadn't! Amina hadn't talked to her about it at all.

"We could go ice skating!" Amina went on, beaming at their parents. "Or maybe just to the cinema and then go for pizza? And can we have a sleepover? With someone to come and do our nails and things? I've made a list of who we want to invite."

"Er…" Dad turned round from the hob looking worried.

"That's a bit more of a grand plan than we were expecting," Mum said gently. She looked down at the list that Amina had pushed in front of her and frowned slightly. "You've only been at school three days, how can you know so many girls?"

"I know everybody," Amina said, waving this away. "Mum, we have to have a really good party *because* we've only just got there. It needs to be perfect!"

"Zara hasn't said anything," Dad pointed out.

"She wants the same as me," Amina said swiftly.

Zara reached down and scooped Pixie into her lap. Stroking the kitten's smooth fur made her feel a bit less panicky inside. She leaned over a little so she could see the list that Mum was looking at. Lucy, Harini, Elysha, Iris, Mia... Lots and lots of names – but Billie wasn't on there.

Amina hadn't even asked her who *she* wanted to invite – to a party that was meant to be half hers.

"No, I don't," she said softly.

Amina whirled round to stare at her. "Of course you do!" She looked utterly shocked – as if she couldn't understand what was happening.

"You never said anything to me," Zara told her. "And my friend isn't on that list."

"What friend?"

"Billie."

"Oh." Amina wrinkled her nose.

"Her. I don't want to invite Billie."

"That's not very nice!" Mum looked at Amina in surprise and she shrugged.

"You just don't like her because she doesn't make a big fuss about you like the others," Zara said.

Amina looked stunned, and Mum and Dad were both staring at Zara now as if they couldn't believe what they were hearing. Zara kept on running her hand down Pixie's soft back. She wasn't sure she could believe it either. Pixie purred and flexed her claws on the furry onesie.

Mum smiled. "So we'll definitely ask Billie to the party. Any more ideas? Not quite so grand and expensive?"

Pixie was scrambling up the front of Zara's onesie now. Luckily the onesie was nice and thick, and Pixie ended up perched on Zara's shoulder looking pleased with herself. Zara was mostly thinking about how funny and sweet she was, so she said what she actually felt, instead of just agreeing to go with what Amina wanted.

"Um… Can we just have a couple of friends round here and have a really nice cake? Maybe a cat-shaped one?"

Amina sighed loudly. "A cat cake would be cute but we want a party everyone's going to remember!"

"I don't." Zara suddenly realized Pixie had stopped purring.

"You don't understand!" Amina said, her voice starting to rise. "It's got to be special! It *has* to be!" She smacked her hand down on the table with a bang.

Zara flinched and Pixie panicked and dug her claws in, hard enough that it hurt.

"Ow, Pixie, gently… I still don't see

why we've got to have such a special party!"

"Oh! You don't understand anything!" Amina hissed and she jumped up and dashed out of the room, leaving Zara staring after her.

Pixie snuggled close up against Zara's onesie as Zara climbed the stairs. She didn't really understand what had happened earlier on, but she'd known that something was wrong when Zara twitched so suddenly. She'd clung on as hard as she could, worried that she was going to slide off – and then she'd heard Zara gasp and Amina go running off upstairs.

For a moment, Pixie had thought Zara was angry but then she'd reached up and unhooked Pixie from her onesie very gently. She'd smoothed down the kitten's ruffled fur and whispered to her. She'd spent ages scratching the exact itchy spot under Pixie's chin while Pixie closed her eyes and almost purred.

But only almost, because she could tell that something was still not right. There was a strange, uncomfortable silence in the kitchen. Even when the family were eating dinner – with Pixie still on Zara's lap, sniffing hopefully at the food and maybe getting a little piece of fish every so often – no one was chatting the way they usually did.

After the meal, Zara carried her

upstairs and rolled
a jingly bell across
the bedroom
floor for Pixie
to chase. But
she didn't
seem to be
trying very
hard, and all
the time Amina
was there, curled up
on the other bed instead of
joining in. Pixie kept stopping
to look over at her, knowing she
wasn't happy – and Zara wasn't either.
When the ball rolled right under
Zara's bed, Pixie and Zara both went
under there to get it – and somehow
they didn't come out again. Zara

stayed curled up against the wall and Pixie snuggled up next to her. It was quiet and dark under there, with Zara's duvet half hanging down.

Zara only wriggled out from under the bed when Mum came up to turn the girls' light off. Pixie had expected Mum to carry her downstairs to her basket in the kitchen – that was what had always happened before, but this time she just stroked Pixie's ears, and hugged Zara and Amina, and left, leaving Pixie sitting on the end of Zara's bed.

"Mum says you can sleep up here tonight," Zara whispered, and there was a grumpy sniff from the other bed. "But I've got to take you downstairs if you don't settle."

Zara was lying down now but the kitten could feel she wasn't asleep – she was watching. Pixie wobbled her way up next to Zara's shoulder.

"I promise I won't roll on you," Zara whispered, and she sounded pleased. "Goodnight, Pixie." And she added, a little sadly, "Night, Amina."

Pixie could just hear Amina muttering, "Night," from the other side of the room.

Chapter Five

Even though Amina had calmed
down, and they were talking again by
the next day, Zara knew that things
weren't back to normal. She wasn't
used to being at odds with Amina –
it made her feel weird and twitchy.

Mum and Dad had explained to
the girls that moving house had been
expensive and a really big party just

wasn't going to happen. In the end they'd settled on something a lot like the party Zara had wanted. Amina seemed to have snapped out of her strange mood but Zara could tell she was still disappointed.

Mum had found someone to make a beautiful cat cake and she'd also ordered cat-shaped invitations, which Dad helped Amina and Zara to write out. Their parents said that six friends was enough – which meant five friends for Amina, and Billie, but Zara was OK with that. The other five girls seemed nice enough, even though she hadn't spoken to them much.

"I wasn't sure if you really meant it," Billie said, when Zara gave her the invitation on Wednesday.

"You – you do want to come?" Zara said worriedly.

"Of course I do!"

"It's just going to be at our house, with pizza and games and stuff…"

"That's much better." Billie nodded. "If it was at the swimming pool or something I wouldn't get to meet Pixie, would I? You're going to have to come to mine some time and see Biscuit too."

Zara felt herself smiling.

But then Billie glanced at the little group around Amina, opening their invitations, and Zara thought she looked worried for a moment. "What's the matter?"

"Nothing…" Billie shrugged. "Just Mia doesn't like me much, that's all. But I can stay out of her way, don't worry!"

Amina dashed past, running to ask Mum something vital about the cake, or the party tea, or the treasure hunt – Zara wasn't sure what. Amina had been wound up all day, too excited to sit still. Now the party was due to start in half an hour, she was non-stop.

Zara felt like curling up with Pixie somewhere quiet and out of the way, but Pixie had sensibly disappeared already. Instead, Zara sat on the stairs, watching the front door and worrying. Would Billie enjoy the party? What if Amina got upset because the party wasn't the way she wanted it to be? So many things could go wrong…

"Do you know where Pixie is?" Amina called as she hurtled into the hallway.

"No… Why?"

"Iris really likes cats, I wanted to show her Pixie. Oh, why isn't it four o'clock yet?"

"It's only five more minutes— Ah, the doorbell!"

"Someone's early!" Amina shrieked, racing for the door. She flung it open

76

and hugged Lucy and a couple of
the others – they must have all come
together, Zara realized. Suddenly frozen
with shyness, she stayed huddled on the
stairs, trying to smile.

"Come into the kitchen! Mum's got biscuits for us to decorate!" Amina squealed and three girls raced after her.

The doorbell rang again and Zara looked round anxiously. No one else was coming to answer it... She brushed imaginary dust off her sparkly skirt and went to open the door, sighing happily as she saw it was Billie waiting on the doorstep with her mum.

"Hello! I brought you a present – and this one's for Amina. Are you OK? You look a bit..."

"Billie..." Her mum made a face. "You look great, Zara. Lovely skirt."

Billie sighed. "I was only going to say you looked worried."

Zara beamed at her. "A bit nervous,

that's all. But I'm not now. Thank you for the presents!"

Suddenly, it felt like the party was going to be OK.

Pixie snapped awake. She'd been dozing, snuggled up in one her favourite hiding places – the bookcase in the living room. There was a tall book leaning over that made a perfect kitten hidey-hole. But now there were footsteps clattering past and high, excited voices.

"It's in here, it's got to be! Look, there, behind the curtains!" Amina whirled in, snatching a piece of paper from the windowsill and a crowd of girls leaned over her to look at it.

"The next clue's in the garden," one of the girls yelled and they all raced off again, leaving Pixie blinking and confused, the fur standing up along her spine.

"We could just let them go and find it," someone suggested quietly. "I don't mind if I don't win any treasure. And it's so windy out there today, I'd rather stay in!"

Pixie edged forwards a little. She hadn't realized there was still anyone in the room.

"Me neither."

Zara and another girl were standing by the sofa, quite still. They didn't look nearly as loud and worrying as the others. Pixie stepped slowly out from her hiding place.

"Hey…" Zara tapped the other girl's arm. "Billie, look. I thought Pixie was hiding upstairs because everything was too noisy but she's here."

"Awww. She's got a little nest in the bookcase!"

"She has hiding places all over," Zara said, crouching down and holding out her hand. "She's so tiny, she can squeeze in anywhere. Dad found her in the pan cupboard yesterday. Pixie, come on… Come and meet Billie…"

Pixie padded cautiously across the carpet to nestle against Zara's hand and then she sniffed Billie too. She could smell another cat on Billie but she hadn't met enough other cats yet to be nervous. It was just interesting. She licked at the girl's fingers. Billie laughed. "I forgot how small kittens are – and Biscuit's got so much fur I don't think he ever looked that teensy. Can you smell Biscuit, is that why you're licking me?"

Pixie closed her eyes as Billie stroked around her ears and then tickled under her chin. She liked this girl.

"If you don't mind missing the treasure hunt, we could take Pixie up to my bedroom," Zara suggested. "Pixie, come on, want to come upstairs?" She stood up, patting her leg and making *puss-puss-puss* noises, and Pixie followed her and Billie out to the stairs.

"Can she get all the way up there?" Billie asked.

"I think she probably could if she really wanted to but usually I just let her do a couple of steps and then I carry her. She's growing so fast though. Soon she'll just race up."

Pixie hopped up the first step, scrabbling to get her back paws on, and then looked hopefully at Zara.

"See! She knows I'll carry her!" Zara leaned down and scooped Pixie up. "Come and see our room – Mum made us tidy it for the party."

The two girls sat on the floor, leaning against Zara's bed, and Pixie clambered around them, chasing a piece of sparkly ribbon that had come off one of

Zara's birthday presents the day before. It bounced and twirled as Zara shook it and Pixie did huge leaps into the air trying to catch the end.

"She's so funny," Billie gasped, out of breath from laughing. Pixie slumped down on her stripey leggings. She kept just missing the ribbon and she was worn out.

"Awww, Pixie. Here you go." Zara laid the ribbon in front of her nose and Pixie rolled over, scrabbling at it fiercely with all four paws. Then she stopped, frozen and peering at the door.

Someone was thumping up the stairs.

Chapter Six

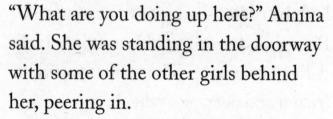

"What are you doing up here?" Amina said. She was standing in the doorway with some of the other girls behind her, peering in.

"We're just playing with Pixie." Zara looked at her sister in surprise. She wasn't sure what Amina was so annoyed about.

"The party's downstairs!" Amina

had her arms folded now and she looked cross. "We're doing the treasure hunt!"

"I know, but me and Billie couldn't see what the clue said and you took it with you…" Zara's voice faltered a little bit as she saw Amina scowl. "We didn't mind!" she added quickly. "I wanted to show Billie our room, and Pixie…"

Amina came further into the bedroom, staring down at Zara and Billie. "You're spoiling our party! And I wanted to show Pixie to *my* friends too." She looked strange, Zara thought. Her eyes were big and shiny with unhappiness, almost as if her feelings were hurt. But that didn't make sense.

"Hey…" Billie said, gently steadying

Pixie as the kitten wobbled to stand up, clearly startled by Amina's sharp voice. "Zara hasn't done anything."

"Mind your own business!" Amina said, glaring at her. "I'm talking to my sister, it's nothing to do with you!"

"I bet Billie made her come upstairs," one of the others said from the doorway. Zara still mixed them up but she was pretty sure it was Mia. "That's just the sort of thing she'd do." There was a nasty little smirk on her face. Zara glanced at Billie and saw that she looked sad – really sad, as though she thought Zara might be about to agree and say it was all her fault. Very gently, Billie put Pixie on to Zara's lap instead. So she could get up and go home, Zara realized. Pixie had her ears flattened down and she looked miserable too. Mia and Amina had upset Billie *and* Pixie.

"She did not! Here." She handed Pixie back to Billie and the kitten let out a worried little mew. "You look after her. I said I wanted to come upstairs because you all ran off and didn't let us join in. Don't you dare speak to my friend like that!"

Mia looked quite surprised that Amina's shy sister was suddenly standing there talking back at her – but it was nothing compared to how shocked Amina looked.

Mia's mouth twisted in a sneer. "I can see why Billie wants to be friends with *her*," she said, nudging Amina with her elbow as though she expected her to agree.

Zara blinked. She couldn't help wondering what they'd been saying about her and Billie when they *weren't* there to listen.

Amina shifted from foot to foot, looking uncomfortable, but Mia was watching her, waiting for her to agree – and at last she nodded.

Zara caught her breath. "Get out of my bedroom!" she snapped.

"I think everyone needs to get out of this room," Mum said, from behind Mia and the others. "Right now."

Everyone slunk back downstairs, looking embarrassed. Some of Amina's friends were giggling but Amina had dark flushed patches across the tops of her cheeks. Which always meant she was upset…

"I'm really sorry," Zara whispered to Billie, who was walking down in front of her, still cuddling Pixie. "Amina – she's – she's not usually mean," she added, shrugging helplessly. Amina wasn't, was she? Zara didn't think so. Amina was always telling her what to do, but not to be horrible, just because Zara wasn't very good at making decisions for herself. Zara had never known her speak to anyone the way she had to Billie.

Maybe she doesn't like it that I've got a friend of my own, Zara realized as they followed Mum into the kitchen where the pizzas were laid out on the table.

"It's OK." Billie half-smiled. "I told you Mia didn't like me. She probably said something to Amina." Then she nudged Zara and her smile turned into a proper one. "I've never seen anyone stand up to Mia like that before!"

Zara tried to smile back. When she'd been telling Mia to leave Billie alone she'd felt brilliant, as if she was unstoppable and didn't care what anybody said. Now that was all seeping away and she was shaky and miserable instead.

Amina was talking and laughing with the others but Zara was sure she was still angry too – that was why she was being so loud and over the top. Zara looked away from her, trying to cheer herself up by feeding a bit of chicken from her pizza to Pixie. She didn't feel like eating much of the slice herself. She wasn't hungry at all.

Zara just wished that Mum would bring out the cat cake she'd been looking forward to so much. It wasn't that she actually wanted any cake, but the birthday cake was supposed to be the last thing – and then the party would be over.

And when it's over, I can tell Amina she ruined it, Zara thought suddenly. It was scary, feeling like this, but she'd had enough of Amina getting everything her own way.

When Mum finally brought out the beautiful cat cake – which did look just like Pixie – Zara managed to blow out the candles without yelling at Amina or throwing icing in Mia's smug face. But when they'd finally closed the front door behind the party guests, she folded her arms and glared at her sister.

"What are you looking at me like that for?" Amina growled. "You were the one who went off upstairs and got us in trouble!"

"I didn't! You wouldn't let us join in the treasure hunt, so we did our own thing!"

"Don't start this again," said Mum, sounding exhausted. "I was ashamed of you both. After all the work Dad and I put in to your party, how could you behave like that?"

"It was Amina!" Zara yelled furiously. "It was supposed to be my party too, not just hers! I had one friend and Amina was horrible to her!"

"You yelled at Mia! Why are you allowed to be mean to my friends?"

"Be quiet!" Dad said. "Zara, go

upstairs to your room. Amina, go to the living room, since you obviously can't be together."

Zara could feel tears choking her throat. How could Mum and Dad not see that it wasn't her fault? Amina and Mia had been so rude… She crouched down and picked up Pixie, wanting to take the kitten upstairs and cuddle her for comfort. Pixie didn't feel very cuddly, though. Usually she seemed to like being picked up but now she felt like a bundle of furry wires and Zara heard her hiss faintly. Zara was just about to put her down again when Amina lunged at her.

"You're not having her!" Amina tried to grab the kitten. "You have her all the time! She's mine too."

Zara didn't mean to tighten her grip on Pixie – it was an accident as she tried to dodge out of Amina's way. But the little kitten let out a frightened yowl and then wriggled wildly, scratching Zara's wrists as she struggled to get free. Zara yelped and dropped her, and Pixie shot away from them, her fur standing up all over.

"Now look what you did!" Amina said triumphantly as Zara sank down on the stairs, looking at the bleeding scratches.

"I didn't mean to," Zara sobbed. She really hadn't, of course she hadn't. Pixie must have been so scared, to scratch her like that.

"Let me see," Mum said worriedly. "Oh, Zara. Come on into the kitchen, we need to wash those."

Zara let Mum bathe the scratches, and she could vaguely hear Dad telling Amina off for grabbing at Pixie and being so mean – but she wasn't really listening. She'd been so shocked when Pixie had scratched her, she hadn't seen where the little kitten had run to. She hated to think of her hidden away somewhere, so frightened and upset.

Where had Pixie gone?

Chapter Seven

"I've checked everywhere I can think of upstairs." Dad came into the kitchen, frowning worriedly.

"But – but she has to be upstairs," Zara whispered. "She's nowhere down here. We've looked and looked."

"She'll be here somewhere, Zara, don't panic," Mum said, hugging her gently. "You know she likes hiding herself away. She was scared and she's gone to find somewhere that felt safe, that's all."

"I don't want her to be scared of us," Zara gulped.

Amina sniffed but she didn't say anything. Zara was too worried about Pixie to keep on being cross with her sister. She wished they hadn't fought – it was their own fault they couldn't find her now.

Zara looked round the kitchen again, hoping to see a kitten hiding spot, something they'd missed because it seemed too strange or silly. In one of the kitchen cupboards, maybe? Pixie had climbed in the pan cupboard the other day. But all the cupboard doors were shut tight.

Just as Zara was thinking that,
a gust of wind rattled against the
kitchen window and the back door
out to the garden swung open.
Everyone stared at it.

"Hang on – that wasn't shut?" Mum
asked slowly.

"I suppose when the girls went out to the garden for the treasure hunt no one closed it properly," Dad said, looking outside. "Pixie couldn't have got through it though, even if it wasn't completely shut…"

"But it's windy," Mum pointed out. "If the door's been swinging open and closed we might not have noticed. She could have slipped out."

"She's not allowed out!" Zara wailed. "She's not old enough!"

"She'll probably just be in the garden somewhere," Dad said. "Let's go and look. Don't get upset, Zara."

Amina and Zara hurried out into the garden, both of them calling anxiously, "Pixie! Pixie, where are you?"

Zara was hoping that a small black-

and-white cat would come darting
out of the bushes. Pixie had never
been in the garden – they'd been so
careful to make sure they kept the
doors and windows shut all this time.
But someone had forgotten in the
excitement of the party.

"Zara, look." Zara turned. Amina
didn't sound angry any more – she
seemed to be as worried and frightened
as Zara was. "The gate. If Pixie was
out here, she could have gone round
the side of the house to the front."

Zara stared at the side gate – it
was one of those fancy metal ones,
all twirly bits stuck together. It would
be the easiest thing in the world for
a little kitten to slip through one of
those holes. Thirty seconds later, Pixie

could be out on the road.

Zara glanced round to see that Mum and Dad had come up behind them and they were staring grimly at the gate too.

"Right." Dad let out a slow breath. "Right. OK. We'd better go and look up and down the street."

Pixie burrowed into the pile of softness. She was still trembling, the fur along her spine standing up in spikes. She didn't understand what had been happening – why Zara and Amina had felt so different. There had been something in their voices, a sharpness that had frightened her so much she'd wanted to bite and scratch. And then Zara had squeezed her and she'd panicked... She had lashed out, desperate to get away.

But now she was safe. It was quiet in here, and calm, and warm. The soft things smelled of Zara and Amina, which would usually have been comforting – mostly it still was. There

was just that little edge of worry. She
was so tired. So much had happened…

Pixie yawned and kneaded her paws
against the soft pile. She slept.

Zara dashed along their street,
stopping to look under every parked
car. She hated to think of Pixie out
here all on her own. Their kitten
seemed so tiny – she just wasn't big
enough and grown-up enough to cope
with cars and people – and what about
dogs? Zara stopped, breathing hard.
She hadn't even thought about that.

"Zara, don't go too far!" Mum called.
"Stay where we can see you."

Zara dug her nails into the palms of

her hands. She knew that Mum and Dad were just as keen to find Pixie as she was but it felt like they were going so slowly.

"She could be hiding in any of these gardens," Dad said gently, catching up with her. "We need to call her and give her a chance to come to us."

"What if she tried to cross the road?" Zara asked, her voice shaking.

Dad looked across at the other pavement, chewing his bottom lip. "The road's not that busy..." he said at last, but Zara could see he was worried.

Mum and Amina were further up the street, talking to one of their new neighbours. Dad had mentioned that both sets had popped round to say a quick hello, but they'd hardly seen them since then and it wasn't as if they knew them.

Mum smiled and waved at the elderly man and hurried to catch them up. "Ben says he hasn't seen her. He's been working in his front garden all afternoon, but he might not have spotted her if she'd run past quickly."

"We have to keep looking," Zara said, flinching as a car drove by – so fast.

"Mmm." Mum glanced up at the sky and Zara realized that the streetlights must have come on in the last few minutes. It was getting dark. What were their chances of finding a mostly black kitten in the dark?

"Let's go along the road one more time and call for her," Dad suggested. "We'll cross over and do that side. Stay with me, Zara, OK? I don't want you running ahead now it's getting dark."

They called and called. Zara's heart jumped inside her when there was a rustling from under a clump of bushes. She thought for a second that they'd found Pixie but instead a curious tabby cat came prowling over and jumped up on to the garden wall.

It was so friendly and it wanted Dad and Zara to stroke it, but Zara just couldn't bear to.

"If you see our Pixie, you tell her to come home," Dad murmured to the cat. Zara thought he was trying to cheer her up, but it didn't work.

There were only a couple more houses now – surely they couldn't have gone all the way along the road already?

"Shall we go round the corner?" Zara suggested to Dad, but he looked at his watch and shook his head.

"I don't think we're going to find her, Zara. We'd better head back."

"We can't just leave her out here!" Zara cried. But Mum and Amina were crossing over to them now and Zara could tell from Mum's face that she was going to say the same thing.

"That book we got from the library said that if your cat got lost you should put their litter tray outside," Amina suggested sadly. "It helps them follow their own scent back home."

Zara glared at her. Until now she'd been too worried about Pixie to think much about their fight. But it felt like this was all Amina's fault! If she hadn't

112

been so horrible at the party... And then tried to grab Pixie... Right now Amina looked as though she really needed a hug – but Zara couldn't bring herself to make her sister feel better.

Chapter Eight

Zara had liked hiding away in small, tight places ever since she'd been very little. Something about them made her feel safe and secure, especially when she was upset. She always slept with toys piled around her too. Mum said it was just one of those things that made her *her*. She also said it would be good if Zara could tell someone she was going to disappear off somewhere, or perhaps she could leave her foot sticking out, so she didn't panic everyone.

Zara didn't think about that when they got back to the house. Mum and Dad went into the kitchen to make some tea, and Amina disappeared upstairs, and Zara just couldn't bear the thought of going to bed. She knew she'd only lie there worrying about Pixie – and being angry with Amina. She'd be waiting to feel the soft weight of a kitten snuggled against her foot or curled up behind her knees. She needed some time to be on her own.

They hadn't been living in this house long enough for Zara to find all the best places, but she knew there was a big cupboard in Dad's office, one that filled in the corner under the stairs. At the moment it had boxes in it – stuff that hadn't been unpacked yet. Dad said he had a feeling they'd still have boxes by the time Amina and Zara left home. Zara was pretty sure that even with the boxes there was space for her to curl up in there. There were some toys in one of the boxes too, she thought – Amina's massive cuddly unicorn and her llama. She could use one of them for a pillow.

Zara slipped into the office, noticing vaguely that Dad's desk was covered in presents everyone had brought. The party seemed such a long time ago now. The cupboard didn't quite shut properly because of the way the boxes were piled, but there was still room enough for Zara to huddle herself inside. She could hear the murmur of voices from the kitchen next door, Amina talking to Mum and Dad – and then the front door banging. Probably that was Amina going to put out Pixie's litter tray in the garden. It was a good idea, Zara admitted to herself. She hadn't remembered the book said that. She supposed Amina did care about Pixie, really. Zara leaned up against one of the boxes and sighed – a sigh that seemed to come all the way from her toes. She was so tired.

Her eyes were just closing when she heard faint footsteps padding across the office – and someone else climbed into the cupboard next to her.

"I thought you'd be here," Amina whispered.

Zara gazed at her sleepily. "How did you know? I've never been in this cupboard before."

Amina shrugged. "I just knew. Um... Are you talking to me? I mean – are you still upset?"

Zara sighed. Was she? She didn't even know any more. Eventually she shook her head – and then realized that Amina could hardly see her. "Only a bit. Not like I was... I'm just worried about Pixie. I still don't understand how you knew I was here." She felt Amina shrug.

"I don't know either. I just did. Dad went out to call for Pixie again and Mum's looking for a local Facebook group to post about her being lost. I suddenly thought that I hadn't seen you for a while. And then I remembered this cupboard. Can you shove up a bit? The corner of this box is sticking into me."

Zara shuffled her bottom further in, and reached inside the box of toys to grab something for Amina to lean against. Then she blinked and moved her fingers again, very slowly.

There was soft fur under her hand – not toy fur, but real.

Kitten fur. Warm, silky, *real* kitten fur.

"Pixie," Zara whispered, screwing up her eyes and trying to see in the dim light from the hallway. "Pixie, is that you?"

There was a faint, hesitant purr and Pixie butted her head against Zara's hand.

"Pixie's there?" Amina breathed, her voice shaking with relief. "Yes! Oh, Pixie! You're here! You never went outside at all. I bet you've been in this cupboard the whole time." Zara half-laughed. There was a strange, wonderful feeling of lightness inside her as all the worry and panic lifted away. She reached out to grab

Amina's hand so she could touch Pixie too. "There – that's not one of the toys, it's her!"

Amina was now laughing with her. "We've been looking everywhere for you, Pixie."

"I suppose we should go and tell Mum and Dad," Zara said slowly. She didn't want to, though. She wanted to stay here with a sleepy, purry kitten and just breathe for a while. Her and Pixie and Amina.

There was a little thud and Zara looked down as tiny paws padded on to her lap. Her eyes were starting to adjust to the dim light now and she could see Pixie slowly turning round and round. The kitten kneaded at Zara's sparkly skirt with her paws, making herself a comfortable nest. Then she lay down with a thump as though to say she was going back to sleep and she wasn't arguing with anyone about it. So now they had to stay where they were.

"I was so scared when we were out on the street looking for her," Amina said quietly. "I really thought she might have been run over."

"Me too."

"Can I stroke her?" Amina asked.

"She's your kitten too!"

"I know, but … I'm sorry, OK?" Amina rubbed Pixie's ears gently. Then she added, "It's just – I'm not used to you having different friends to me. And you're not even sitting with me in class now! Everything feels weird."

Zara looked at her sister in surprise. Amina was the confident one – she shouldn't care that Zara had moved tables. "It'll be OK," she whispered.

"I suppose. And I suppose Billie's all right. But I thought *I* was your best friend," Amina added, her voice very small.

"You are! But I can still have Billie as a friend too," Zara said.

"I know." Amina was silent for a moment. "I was jealous," she admitted. "But I'll try not to be. And I'm sorry about Mia as well," she added, her voice suddenly going high and surprised. "I knew she could be a bit catty – sorry, Pixie – but she was horrible! And – and I didn't tell her to shut up when she said that stuff about you. I should have done."

Zara was silent. That was what had hurt so much, that Amina hadn't stuck up for her. "I *really* don't like Mia," she said, gently stroking Pixie's paws.

"I don't think I do either," Amina said, her voice very small. "But I wanted everyone to like me. And they all seem to listen to her..."

"Yeah, because otherwise she'll say mean things about them."

Amina nodded her head sadly. "But Lucy's nice and some of the others. I just won't hang around with Mia so much." Then she laughed, sounding surprised, and Zara saw that Pixie had poked Amina with her paws.

The kitten stretched one front paw, and then the other, and then both, and then she stuck her bottom up in the air and wriggled it. At last she yawned, a huge yawn that showed tiny teeth, glinting white in the dim light. Then she went into her padding round and round routine again – this time wobbling between Zara's lap and Amina's, the way she had done the first day they'd brought her home. She slumped down again across both their laps, stretched out as far as she could, as though she was trying to link them together.

Pixie could hear the change in Zara's voice and even more in Amina's. That sharp angry sound had gone. They were sitting close to each other too. She felt the fear that had been sitting deep down inside her ease away and she yawned. She liked this comfortable space with the boxes and the soft things to lie on, but it was even better when Zara and Amina were there too.

She stretched deliciously, feeling all her muscles tense and relax. Then she stood up, pacing over both girls' laps and pounding her paws until everything was just right.

Pixie settled down comfortably, rolling on to her back and showing Zara and Amina the soft whiteness of her tummy. She purred wheezily – half a purr and half a snore – and went back to sleep.

Safe and warm and loved.

HOLLY WEBB

Holly Webb started out as a children's book editor and wrote her first series for the publisher she worked for. She has been writing ever since, with over one hundred books to her name. Holly lives in Berkshire, with her husband and three children. Holly's pet cats are always nosying around when she is trying to type on her laptop.

For more information about Holly Webb visit:

www.holly-webb.com